Harcourt Brace & Company

San Diego   New York   London

Snowballs

Lois Ehlert

Requests for permission to make copies of any part of
the work should be mailed to: Permissions Department,
Harcourt Brace & Company, 6277 Sea Harbor Drive,
Orlando, Florida 32887-6777.

Weather reports on the back cover are reprinted with
permission from the *Milwaukee Journal*.

Library of Congress Cataloging-in-Publication Data
Ehlert, Lois.
Snowballs/Lois Ehlert.—1st ed.
p.   cm.
Summary: Some children create a family out of snow.
Includes labeled pictures of all the items they use,
as well as information about how snow is formed.
ISBN 0-15-200074-7
[1. Snow—Fiction.] I. Title.
PZ7.E3225Sn   1995
[E]—dc20   94-47183

QPONMLKJIH

Printed in Singapore

Do you think birds know when it's going to snow?

I do.
The seeds
we left out
were almost
gone.

New snow
would soon
bury the rest.

We'd been waiting for a really big snow, saving good stuff in a sack. Finally it was a perfect snowball day.

We rolled
three snowballs
and made a
snow dad.

Added a
snow mom

and
a cool
snow
boy.

Made
a snow
girl

and a
round snow
baby.

MKE
MILWAUKEE
Wisconsin

CLAIM CHECK 34-080
See Reverse Side
for Conditions

Built our cat and to end the day,

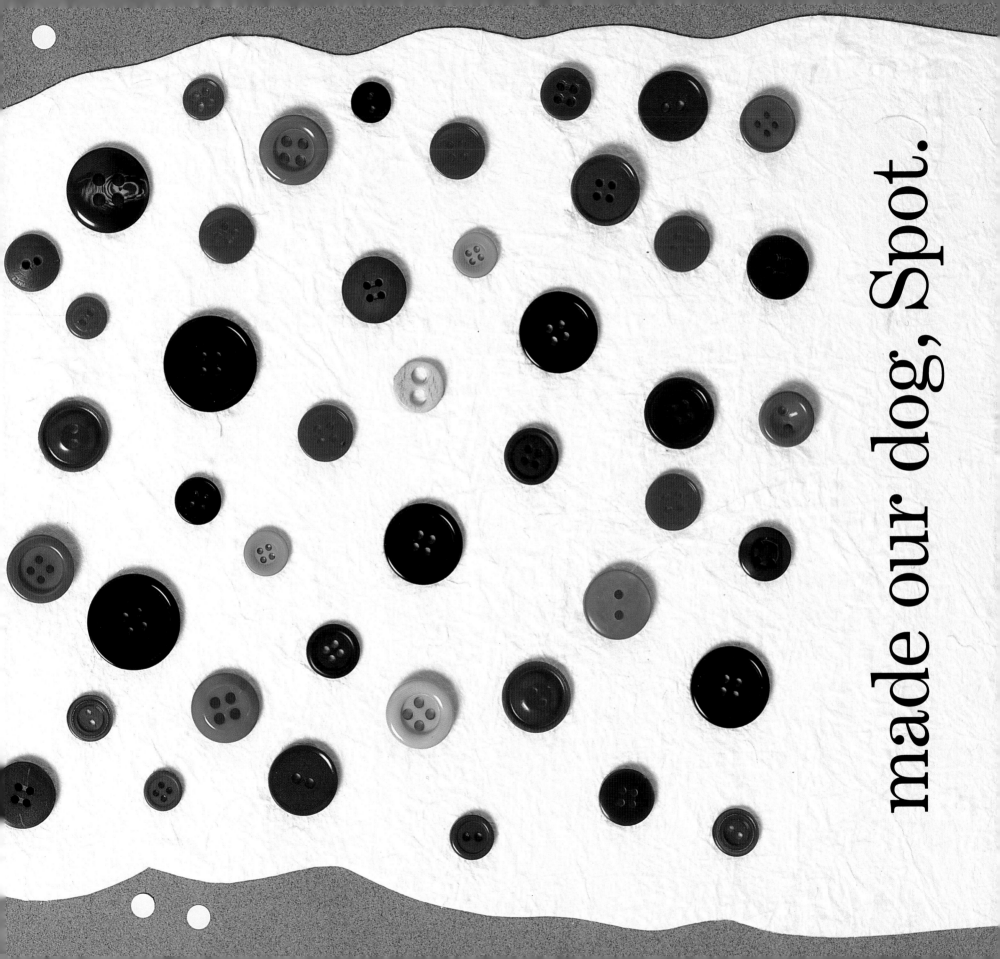

made our dog, Spot.

I guess you you know
what happened
when the sun
came out.

Snow dad's
shrinking.

Mom is mush.
Boy's a blob;
girl is slush.

Baby's melting;
cat's getting small.
Dog is a puddle.

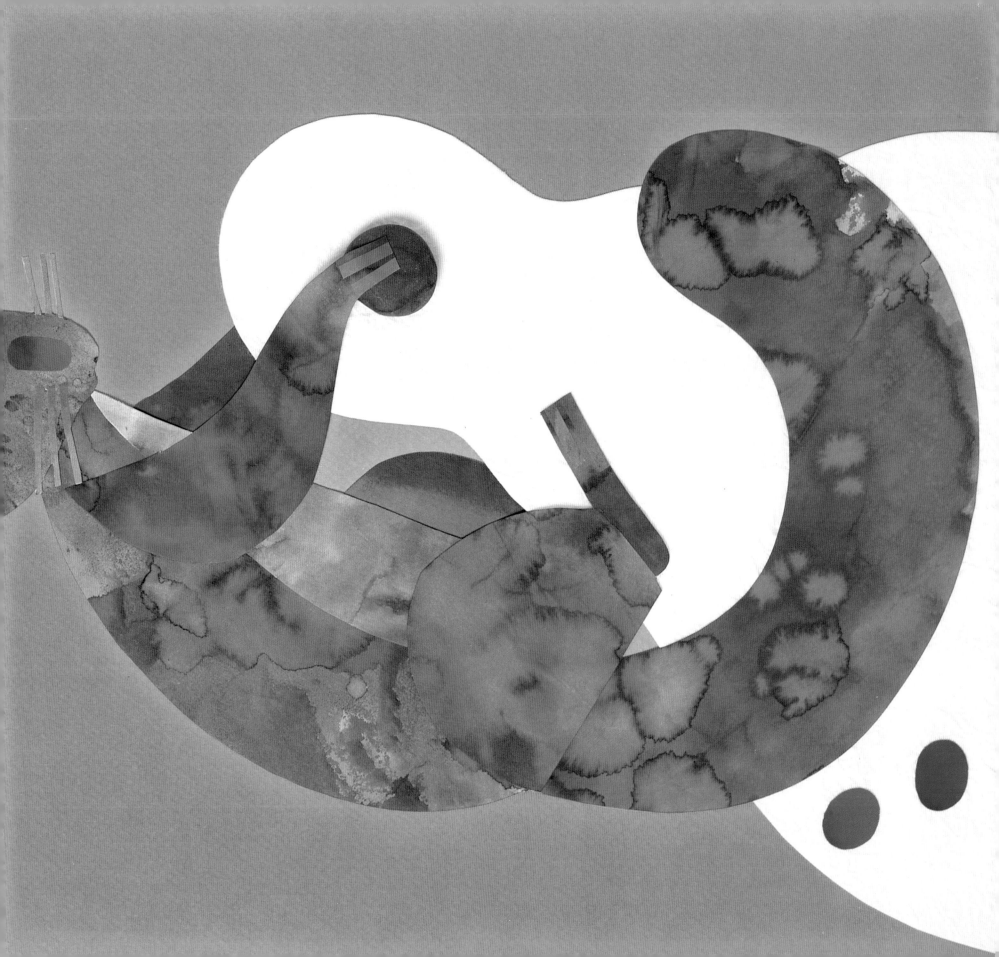

So long, snowball.

good
stuff

toy wheel

twig

seashell

pressed
maple leaf

Japanese stone

Thai appliqué heart

corn

evergreen
branch

foil
candy
wrapper

Guatemalan belt and tie

fork

metal washer

cinnamon stick

CLAIM CHECK

See Reverse Side
for Conditions

34-080

walnut

pencil

toy fish

pine cone

Mexican scrub brush

claim check

button

bottle cap

Bolivian hat

sunflower seeds

toy compass

luggage tag

MKE
MILWAUKEE
Wisconsin

strawberry

cranberry

popcorn

jingle bell

crayon

Peruvian sock

ribbon

twine

screw

Guatemalan purse

peanut

African kente cloth

English silk tie

telephone wire

metal nut

coffee bean

raisin

snow info

clothespin

clothesline

Wisconsin mitten

Korean glove

Italian mitten

Afghani
glove

Wisconsin mitten

What is snow?

Snow is a frozen, solid form of water. Water can take three forms:

gas—droplets dispersed in air, such as steam or fog

liquid—rain, oceans, lakes, streams, rivers, and drinking water

solid—ice, snowflakes, hail, sleet, and frost

What makes it snow?

Although we can't always see the process, water is constantly evaporating from earth, changing from its liquid form to water vapor, its gas form. If you boil water, steam rises as gas. If your windows are cold, steam collects on the glass, cools, turns back into liquid, and water droplets run down your windows.

Imagine this process happening on a much larger scale. Water from our oceans, lakes, streams, and rivers evaporates, or turns into water vapor, which goes into the atmosphere. The water vapor blows around in the wind, clings to bits of dust and salt in the air, and gradually forms a cloud.

When a cloud becomes saturated with water vapor, it releases the droplets and water returns to earth. The temperature in the cloud determines whether it will release rain, snow, or other forms of precipitation, such as hail and sleet. If the cloud is warm, it will rain. If the temperature in the cloud is cold enough, water droplets freeze into ice crystals and snowflakes will fall. If the air below the cloud is warm, the snowflakes melt and fall as rain. If the air below is cool, the snow will continue its journey to earth.

If the earth is warm, snow melts when it lands. If it's cold, snow covers the ground, and that could mean a snowball day—at least until the warm sun comes out and melts the snow. Then the process of evaporation begins all over again.

Photographs are by Lillian Schultz except the three at the far right of this page, which are by Richard Ehlert, and the ones at the top and bottom left of this page, which are by Allyn Johnston.